SPECIAL !

STEVE POWERS

FIRST &

VILLARD | NEW YORK

FIFTEENTH

LOOK!

POP ART
SHORT STORIES

A VILLARD BOOKS TRADE PAPERBACK ORIGINAL

Copyright © 2005 by Stephen Powers

Published in the United States by Villard Books, an imprint of The Random House Publishing Group, a division of Random House, Inc., New York.

VILLARD and "V" CIRCLED Design are registered trademarks of Random House, Inc.

ISBN 0-345-47559-3

Printed in China on acid-free paper

www.villard.com

2 4 6 8 9 7 5 3 1

FOR MARIA AND ROBERT

—

ACKNOWLEDGMENTS

Friday at the Theftway was witnessed firsthand by Leigh Stevens. Ben Woodward and Jesse Geller played Earl and Mark. Tim Badalucco, Kenji Ukigawa, and Sara Fisher played Saul, Waylon, and Cindy. Abe Jaffer and Mike Levy played Cashus and Shah. Nathan Smith played Superfeen; Guess and Wise know who inspired him. Geneiveve at Tom Powel Imaging pored over every pixel. *Waylon Saul* was created thanks to a grant from the Henry Moore Foundation. Always Li Signs framed every piece. Dan Murphy and Mike Levy helped paint every piece. Matt Wright put down a few coats of enamel as well. Maryanne Powers is the muse. Emilie Stewart and Mark Tavani got Superfeen a home. Finally, everybody at the studio would like to thank Kurt Heasley and the Lilys for making great music.

CONTENTS

INTRODUCTION   vi

1 BREAKFAST REVIVAL   0

2 FRIDAY AT THE THEFTWAY   10

3 MARK & EARL   24

4 WAYLON SAUL   50

5 MUTUAL FUNDS   102

6 SUPERFEEN WASTES THE DAY
   AND SAVES THE NIGHT   134

7 FORTRESS   152

8 ENDZONE DANCER   160

LOOK!

INTRODUCTION

Last night I saw my neighborhood crackhead. When our eyes met, I thought the two things I always think when I see him: "How are you not dead yet?" and "Remember that time I kicked you in the stomach?" The crackhead looked at me like I was a court date, and as he reversed his course, I realized these two thoughts are the streets that make up the corner of *First & Fifteenth.*

"How are you not dead yet?" I jog, I yoga; he smokes cocaine and drinks until he pees his pants. I wake up every morning feeling half dead, and he's already up rattling a cup. I come home at night feeling like burnt toast, and he's doing the electric slide in front of my building. He's not a superhero but a super-feen. I never met a superhero, but I know a few superfeens. They crash through walls all night long, and in the morning brush off their shoulders and do it again. I've tried being a drunk and a drug addict; I'm no good at it, I get sad and sick too quick. So I salute the superfeen. There's no mountain of coke too high, no glass of whiskey too deep for him. He's all menace and no penance. He's going to save the day, but he's got to see somebody first.

"Remember that time I kicked you in the stomach?" One night my wife came home upset because she was accosted in the foyer of our building by a man she described as looking like my neighborhood crackhead. I immediately went out looking for him, but he was gone. I caught up to him three days later, asleep on the street, and I kicked him awake. He jumped up to demand an explanation, and I told him not to mess with girls on my street. He was protesting his innocence as he crawled back under his blanket. Chivalry accomplished, I went on my way. Two weeks later, my wife and I are walking down the street. I see the crackhead and say, "That's your guy, right?" She says, "No, that's not him."

Every story in this book is like that: a quick one-act play where the actors meet and play their parts and a punchline drops like a curtain to close the scene. They are the type of stories that get passed around like dollar bills. And like dollar bills, even if you have a lot of them, you don't mind getting more. I started saving them for this book in the spring of 2001, after a trip to Coney Island. I had been painting signs for a little while and Coney Island was a great place to look at old signs and get ideas. I was looking at one sign—a visual riot of words and pictures extolling the virtues of fried foods and malt beverages, by a legend named Henry Wallace—while listening in on a conversation two men were having about an associate who'd been arrested for shoplifting. It was a simple tale of a perfume heist that ended when the bag ripped and the contents broke; the perfume-splattered perp got caught when the cops got a whiff of him. Suddenly the bottles of beer on the sign I was looking at became perfume bottles, and the words changed into the plot of the caper I was hearing. It's a good thing I wasn't overhearing *The Iliad,* or this book would never be finished.

Somewhere nearby, people are living these stories, and where they are happening there are painted signs and dollars to be had. *First & Fifteenth* is a place where people are bad at being good or good at being bad, and the neighborhood is all the better for it.

Steve Powers
New York, New York
Feburary 2005

LOOK!

1

BREAKFAST REVIVAL

O THE FULLEST EXTENT
OF THE LAW!
— MGR

PIGEON

PLEASE BE KIND
& CLEAN THIS
AREA AFTER
EACH USAGE
IT IS NOT
POSSIBLE TO
CLEAN AFTER
EACH PERSON
AMERICAN ENDS WITH I CAN

F
2 L
HAN
MO
CA

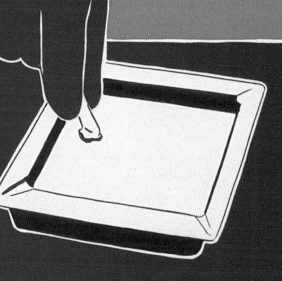

I WILL SNUFF OUT EVIL

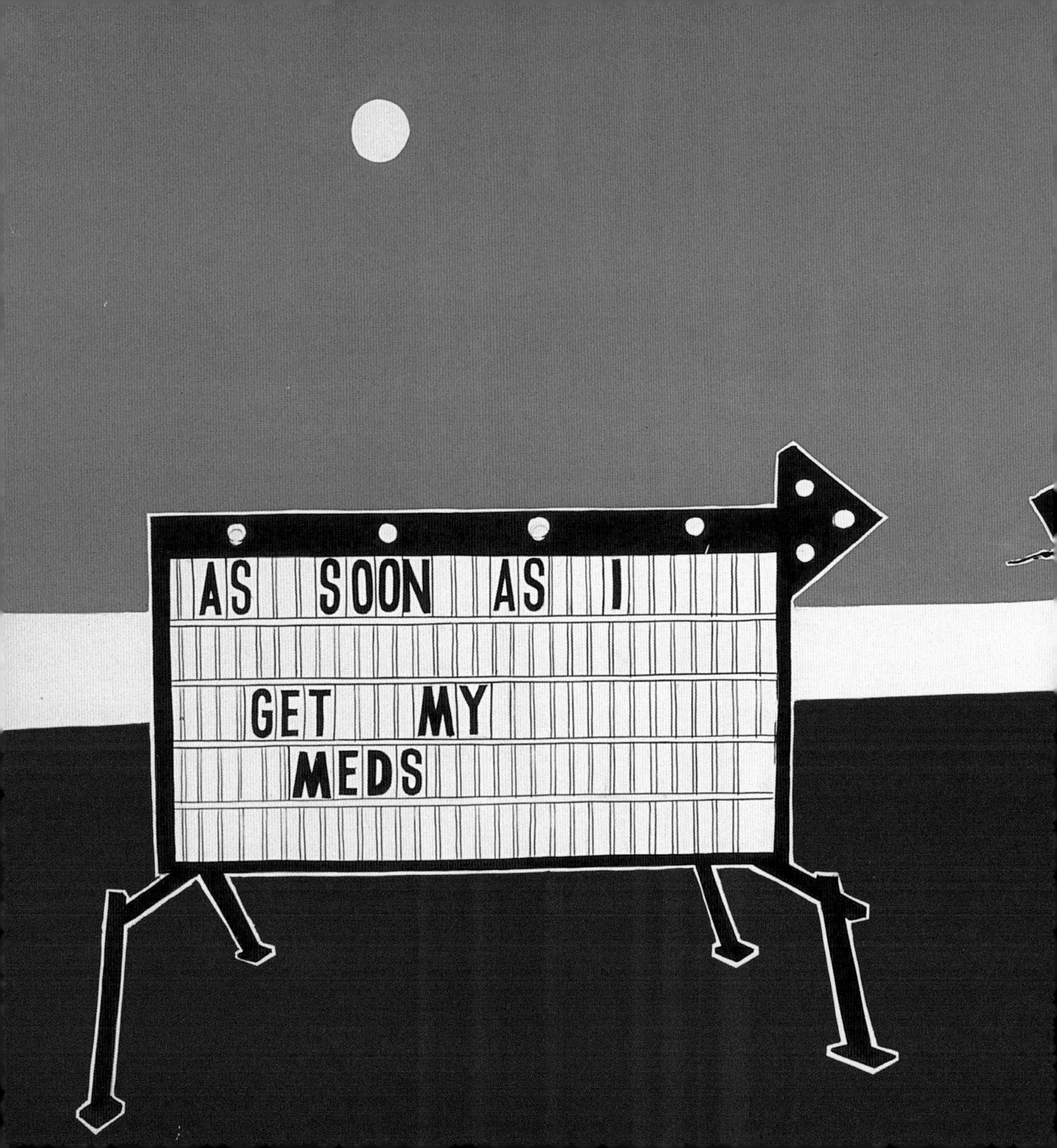
AS SOON AS I
GET MY
MEDS

SPECIAL !

2

FRIDAY AT THE THEFTWAY

O THE FULLEST EXTENT
OF THE LAW!
— MGR

PIGEON

We Prosecute
Shoplifters
TO THE FULLEST EXTENT
OF THE LAW!
— MGR

F
2
HA
MO
CA

EARL
(215) 877
EARL
(215) 877
EARL
(215) 877

15

DISLODGES

A

HAM

17

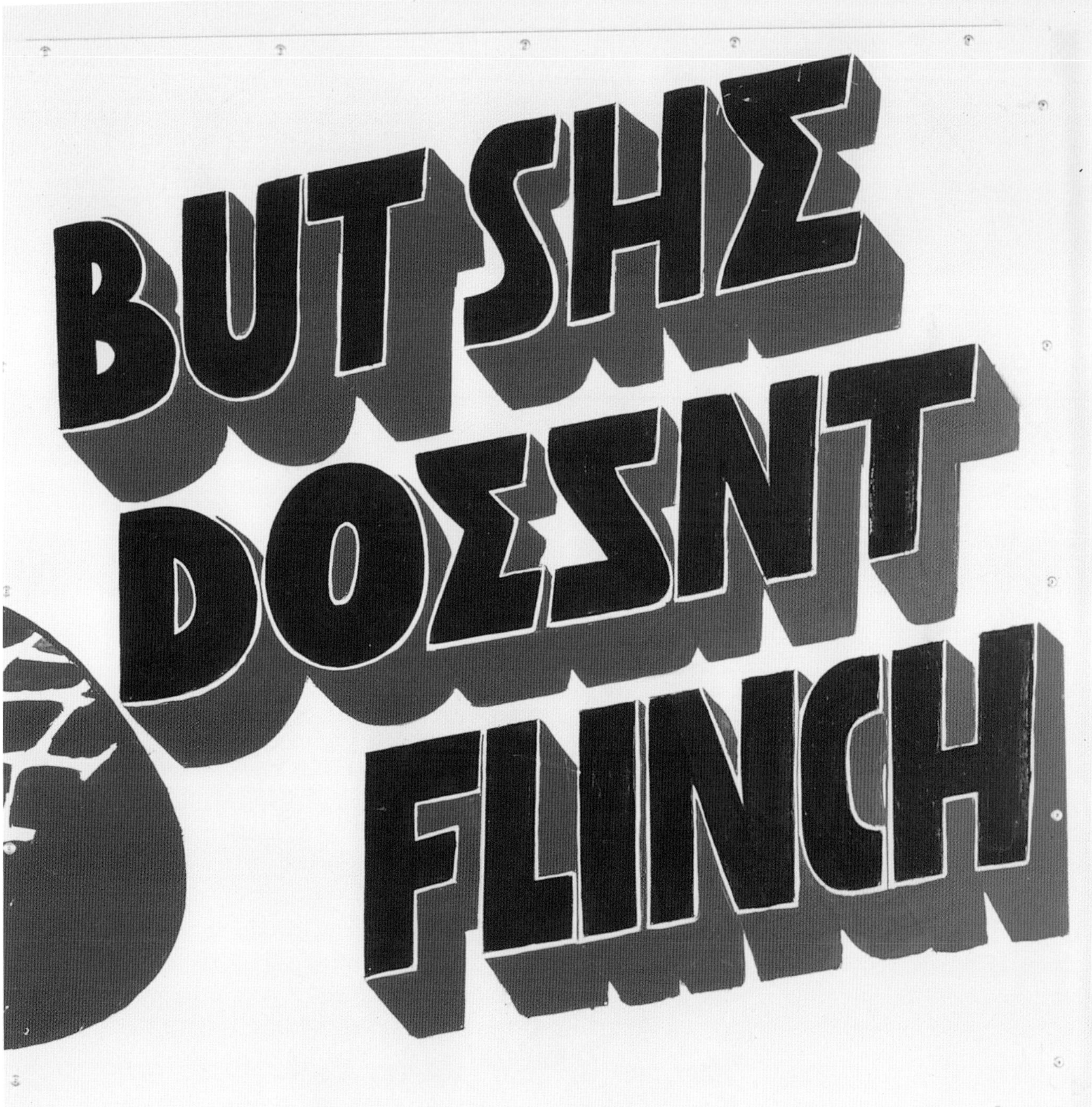
BUT SHE
DOESN'T
FLINCH

LOOK!

3

MARK & EARL

THE FULLEST EXTENT
OF THE LAW!
— MGR

PIGEON

FOR SALE
2 BR, 1½ BATH
HANDYMAN SPECIAL
MOTIVATED SELLER
CALL OWNER

FO

2 L

HAN

MO

CA

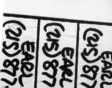

LIKES
ACCIDENT
FRAUD

EARL IS
TODAYS
VICTIM

GAME

THERE'S NO NEED TO NEED TO CALL A COP

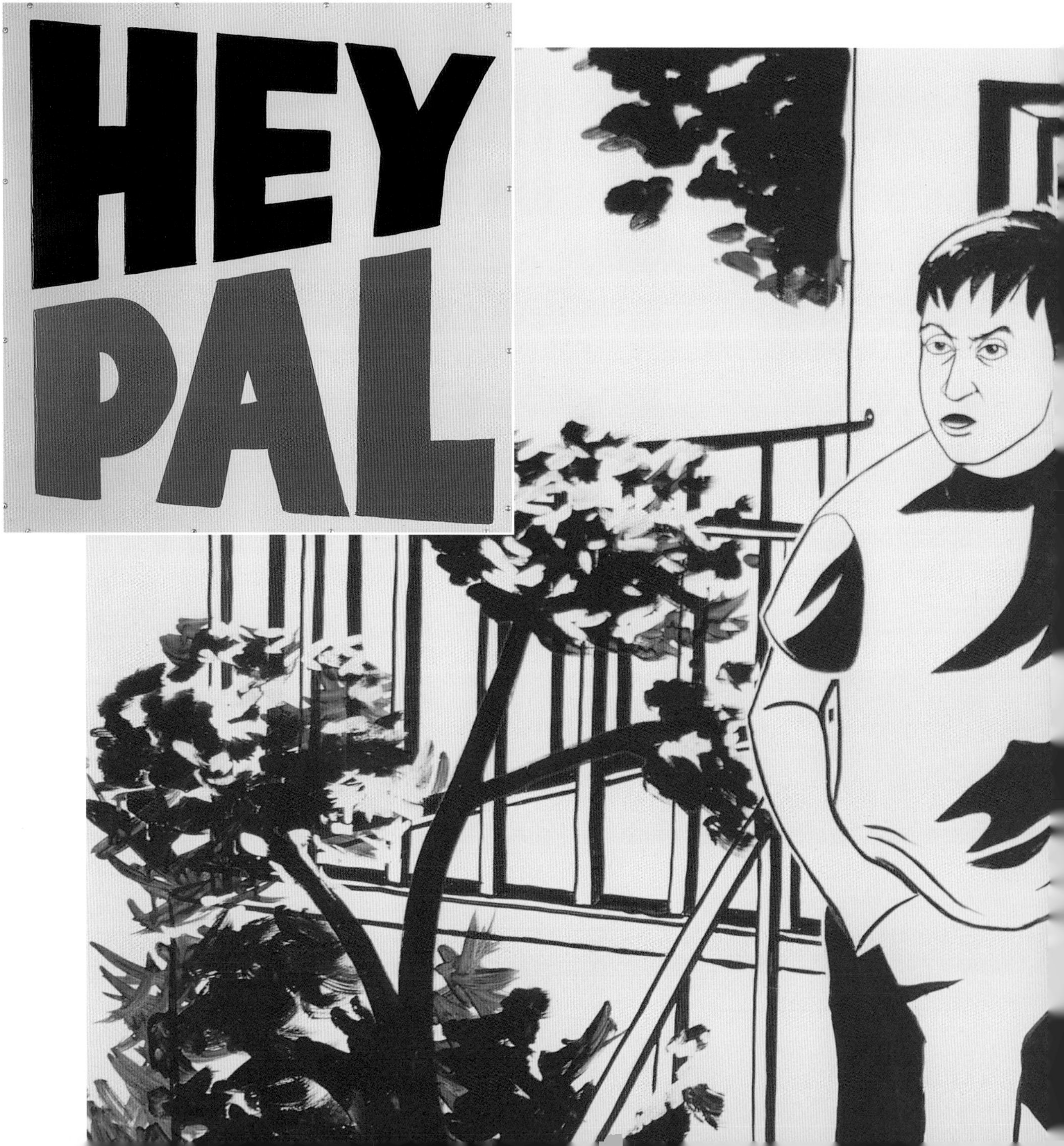
HEY
PAL

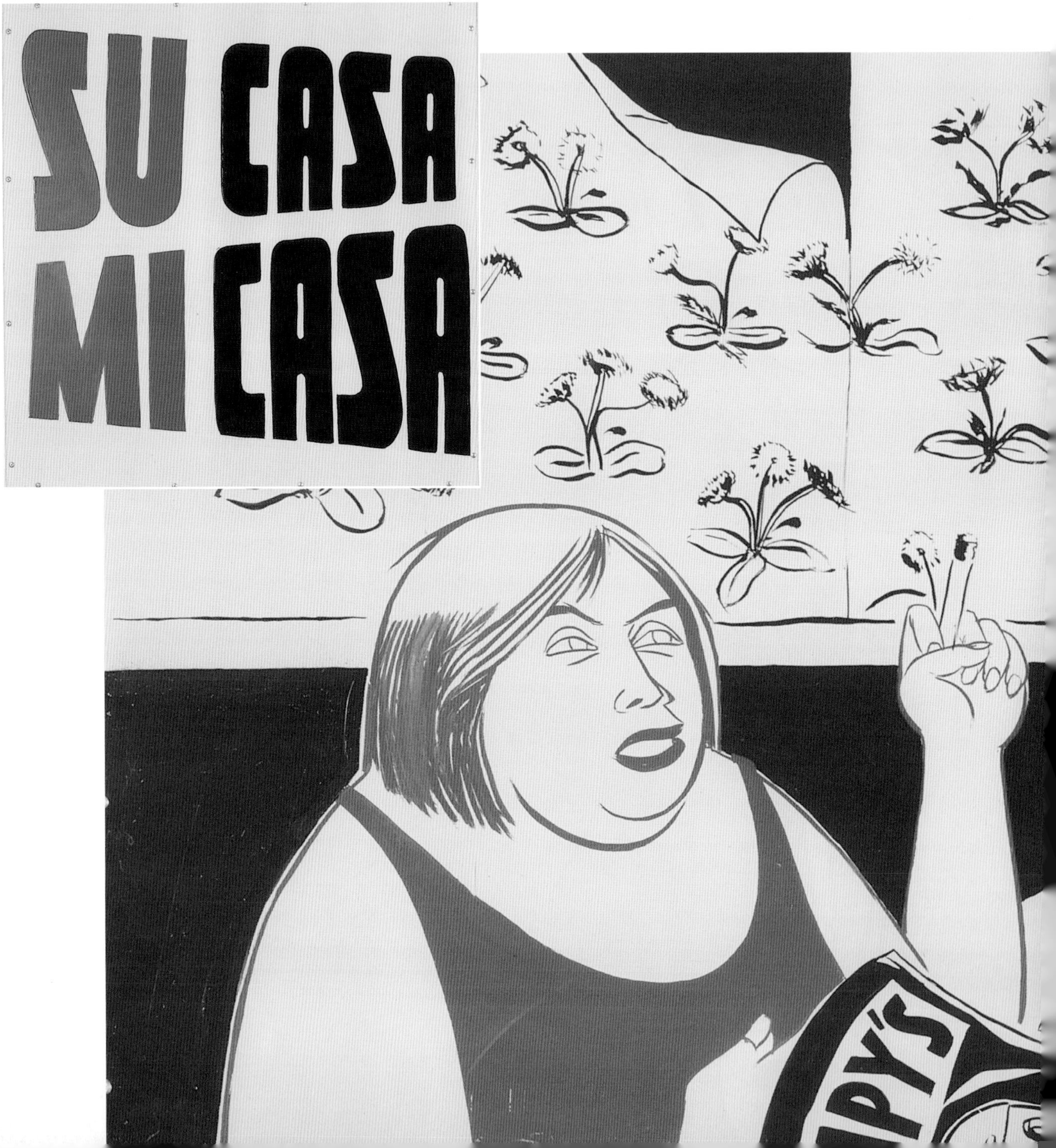
SU CASA
MI CASA

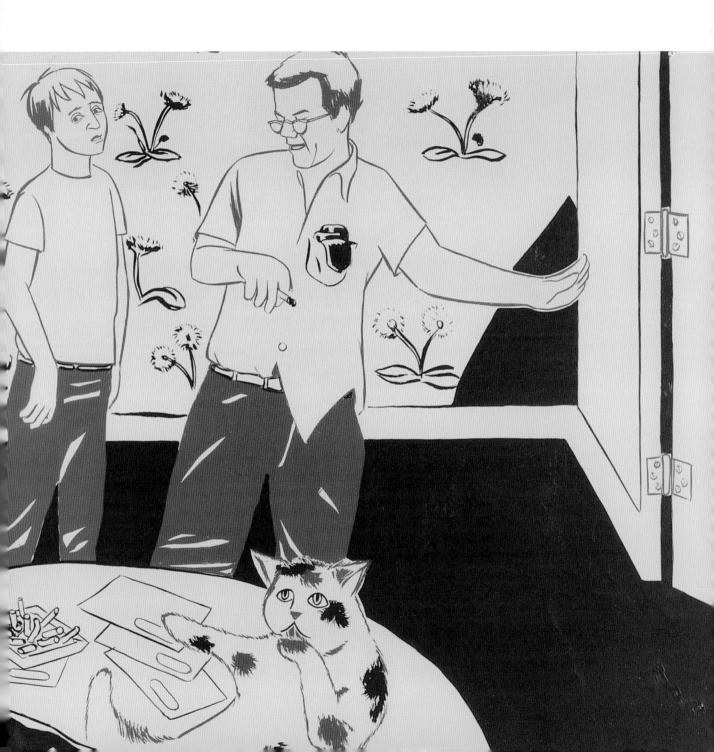

BEFORE THEY DEAL

Mark Folds

SPECIAL !

4

WAYLON SAUL

O THE FULLEST EXTENT
OF THE LAW!
— MGR

PIGEON

NO SKI 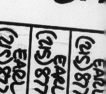 MASK
WE'LL CALL
POLICE

F
2L
HA
MO
CA

WAYLON IS THE WORST

HE PUNCHED CINDY METZER

EXCEPT SAUL GOODE

BUT HE'S A CRIPPLE

AT LEAST HE WAS,

HE GOT HIS

BRACES OFF

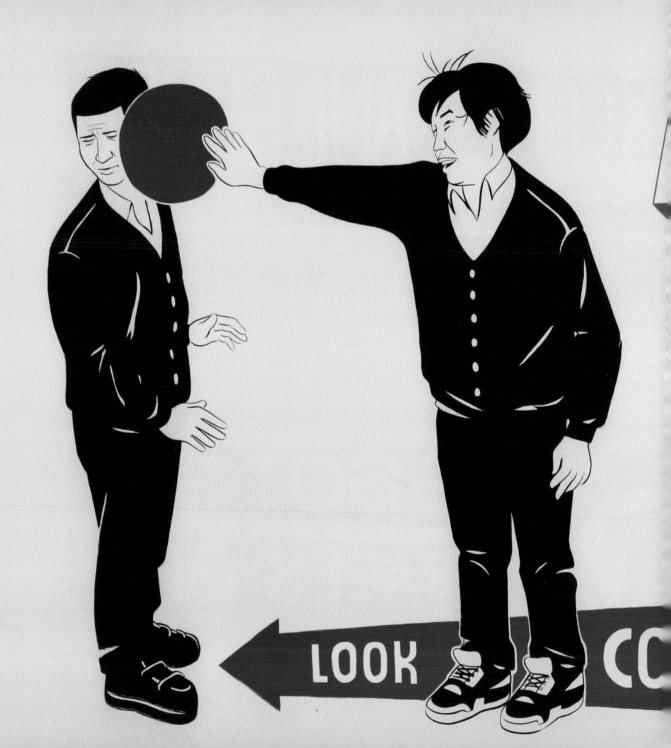

Mr. Ellie

pities
Saul

RECTIVE SHOES

SO HE'S IT IN

DODGE●BALL

SA
I
FA

CINDY

SAUL GOT US ALL WITH THE RED BALL UNTIL THERE'S TWO LEFT TO PURSUE

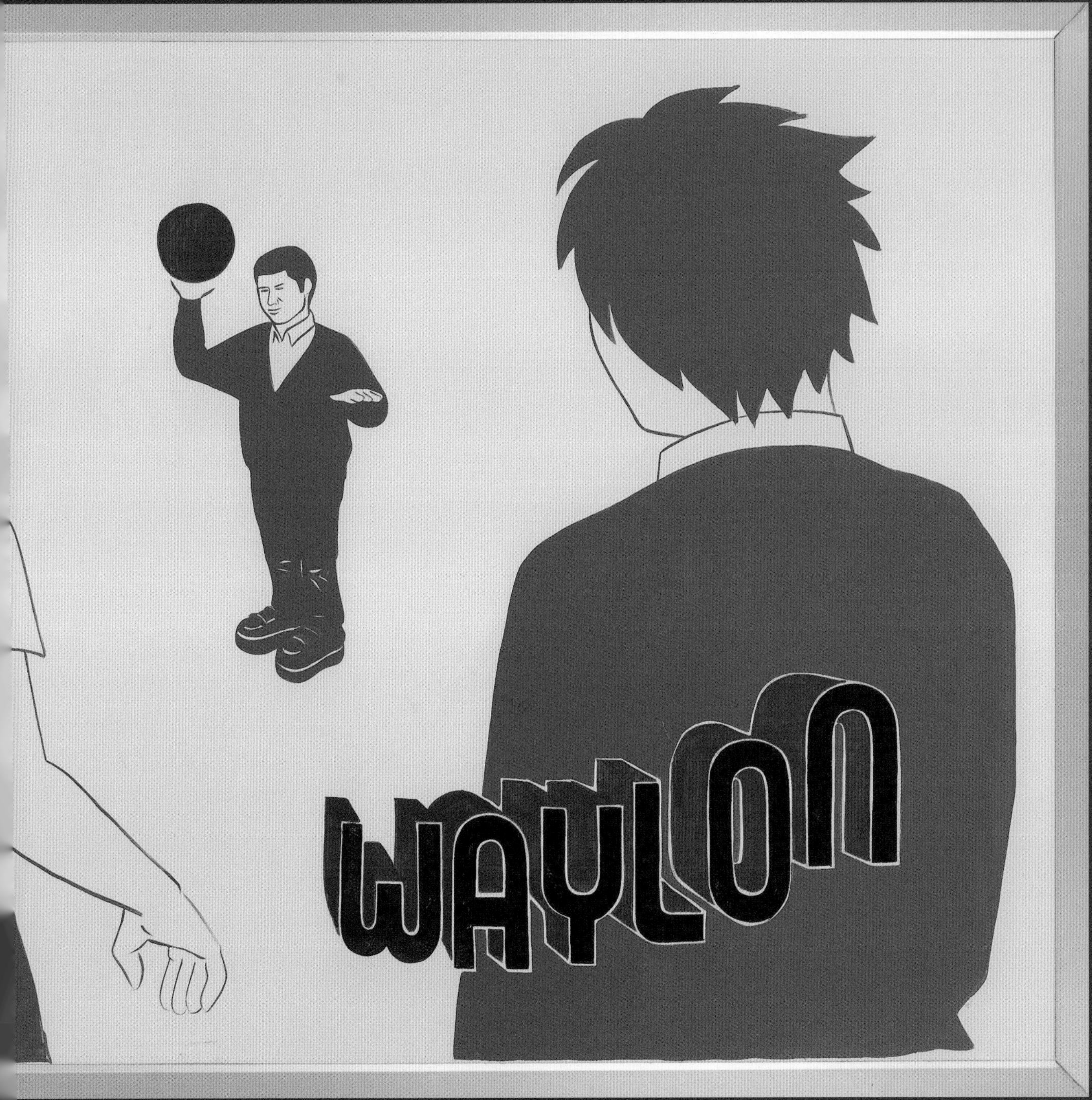
WAYLON

WAYLON WON'T BUDGE
CINDY'S & JUST CUTE

SAUL

W

HE HAS

DOES
at
TO DO

WAYLON CAN'T TAKE IT

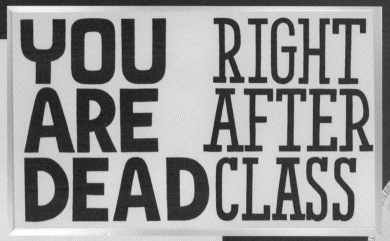

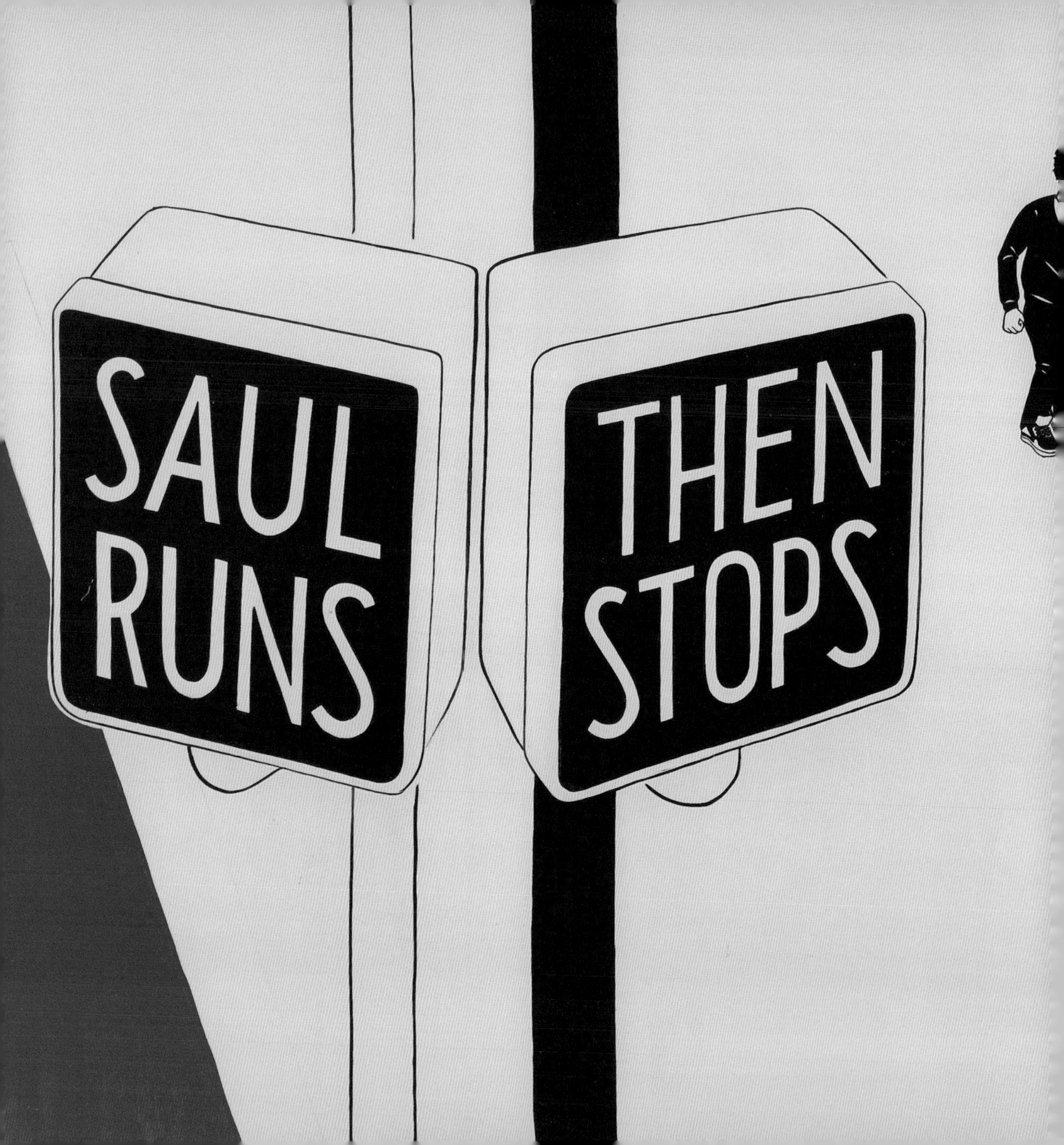
SAUL RUNS
THEN STOPS

SHOES COME OFF

DUKES GO UP

BUT SAUL GETS
WHOOPED

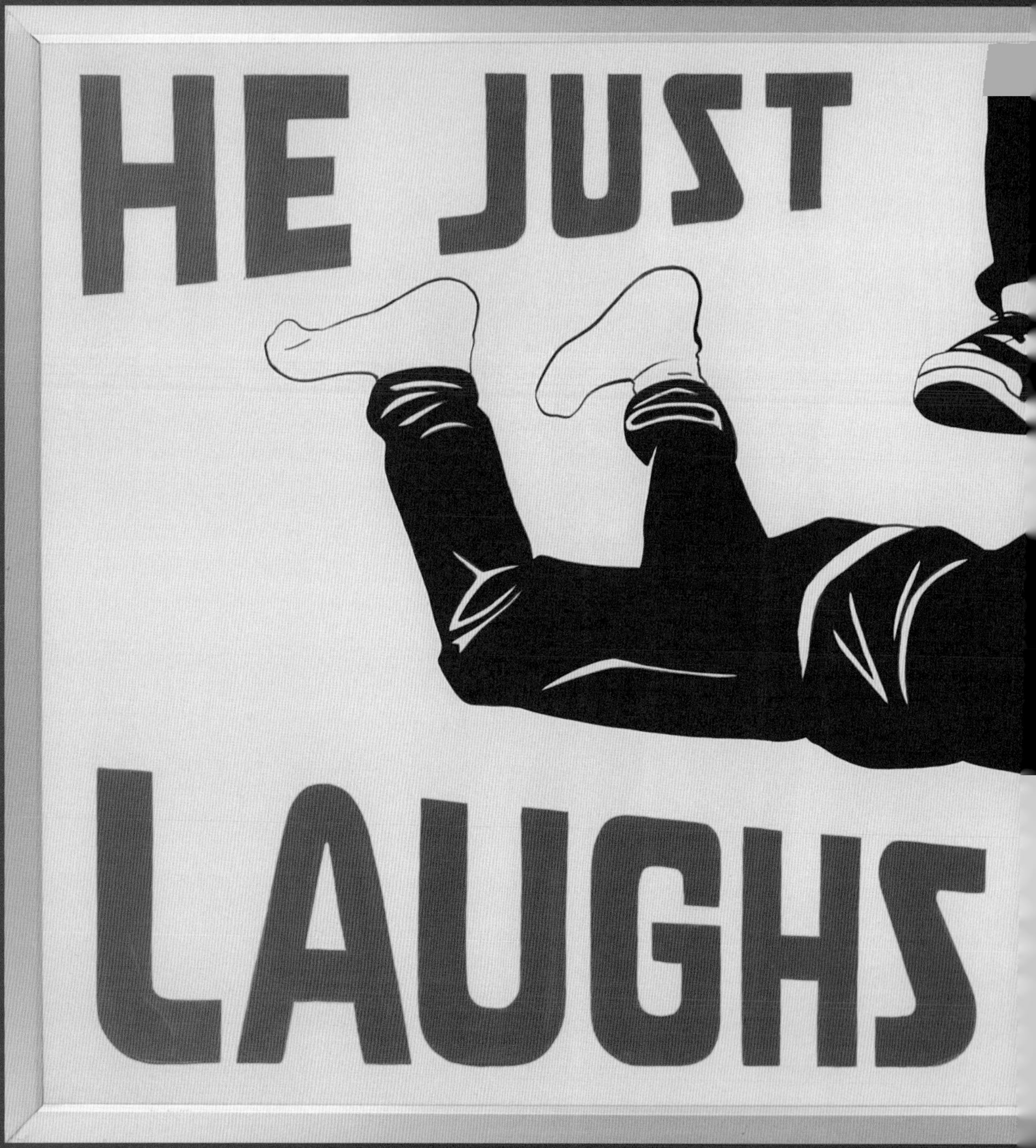
HE JUST
LAUGHS

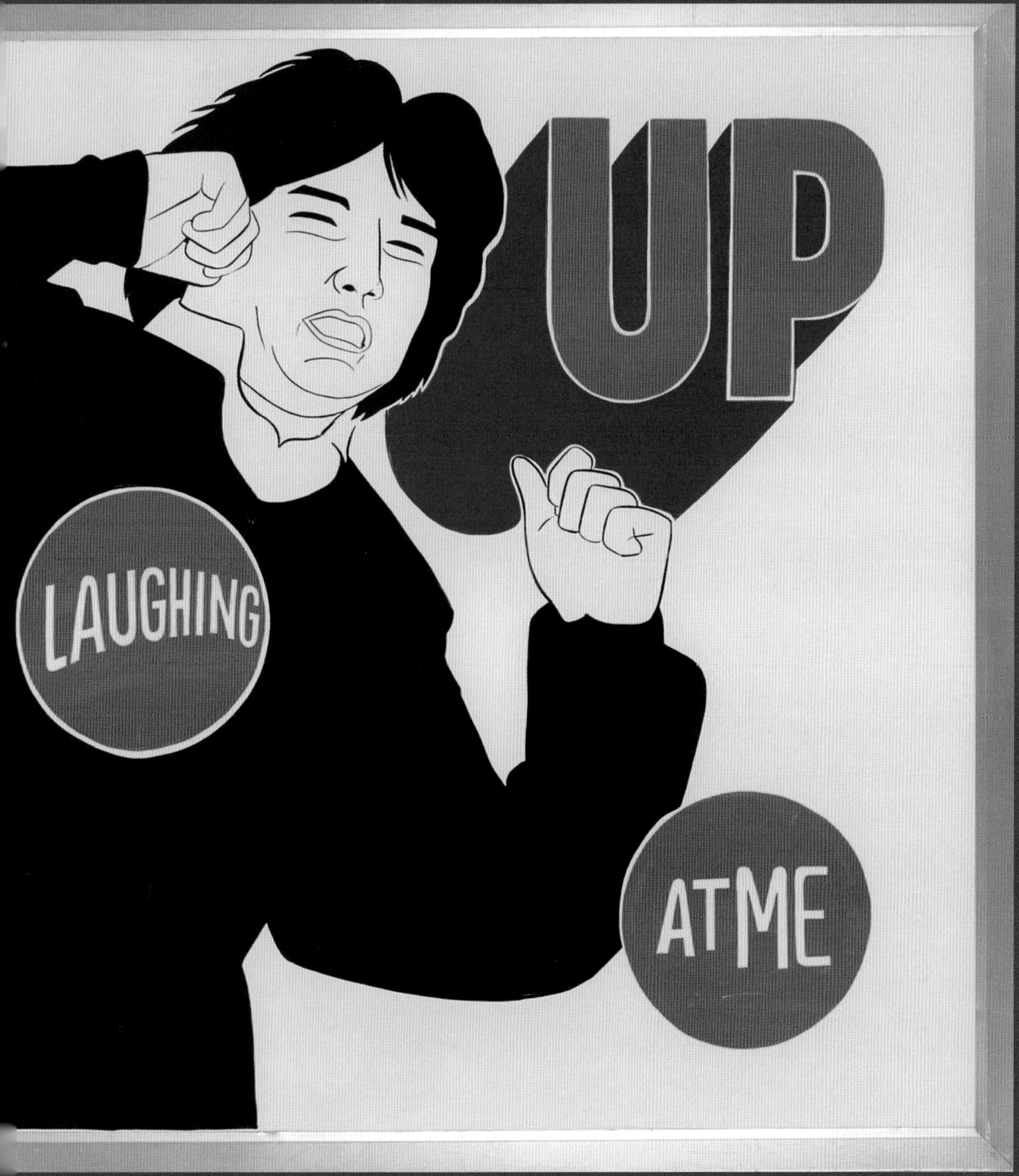
UP
LAUGHING
AT ME

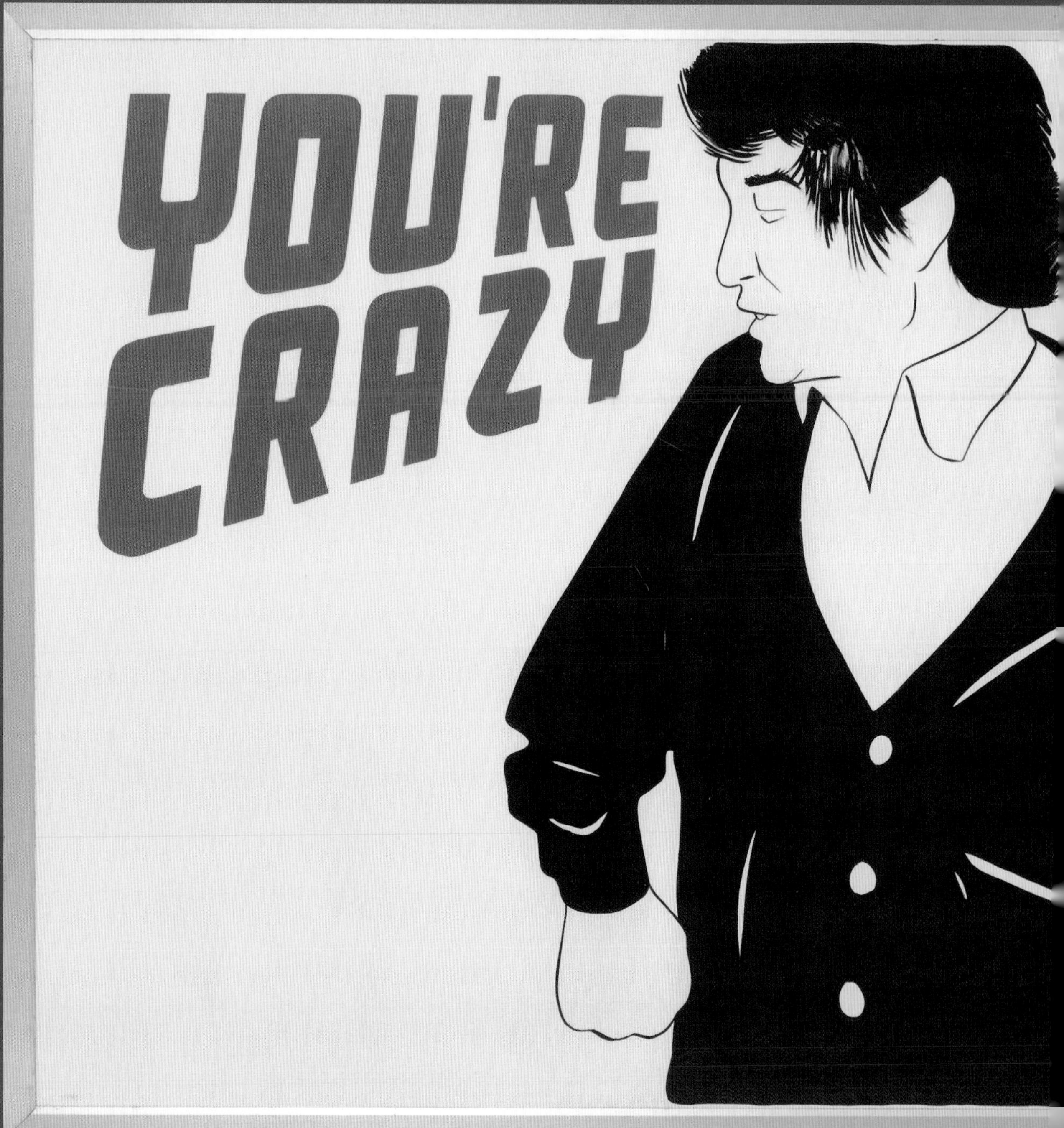
YOU'RE
CRAZY

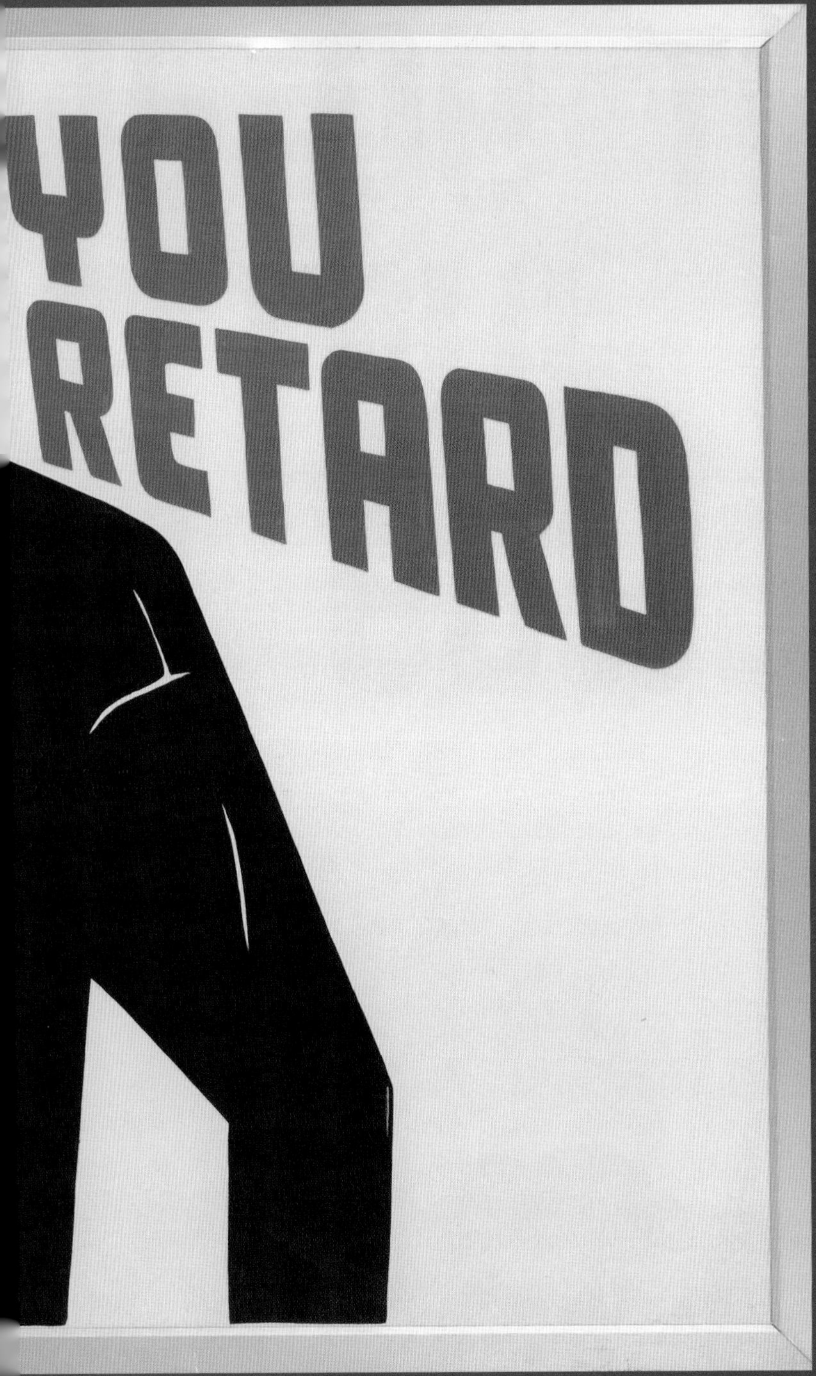
YOU
RETARD

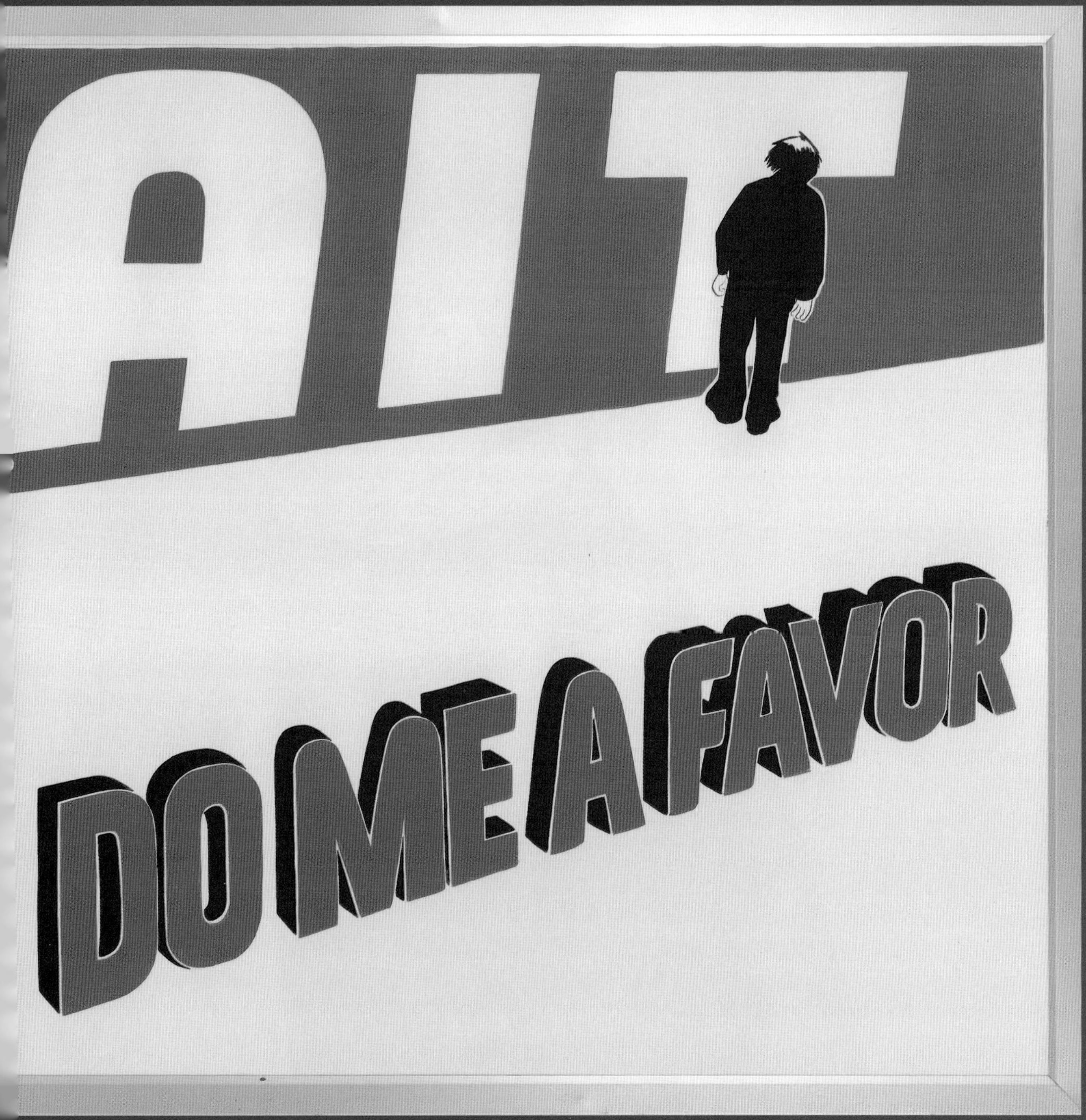
DO ME A FAVOR

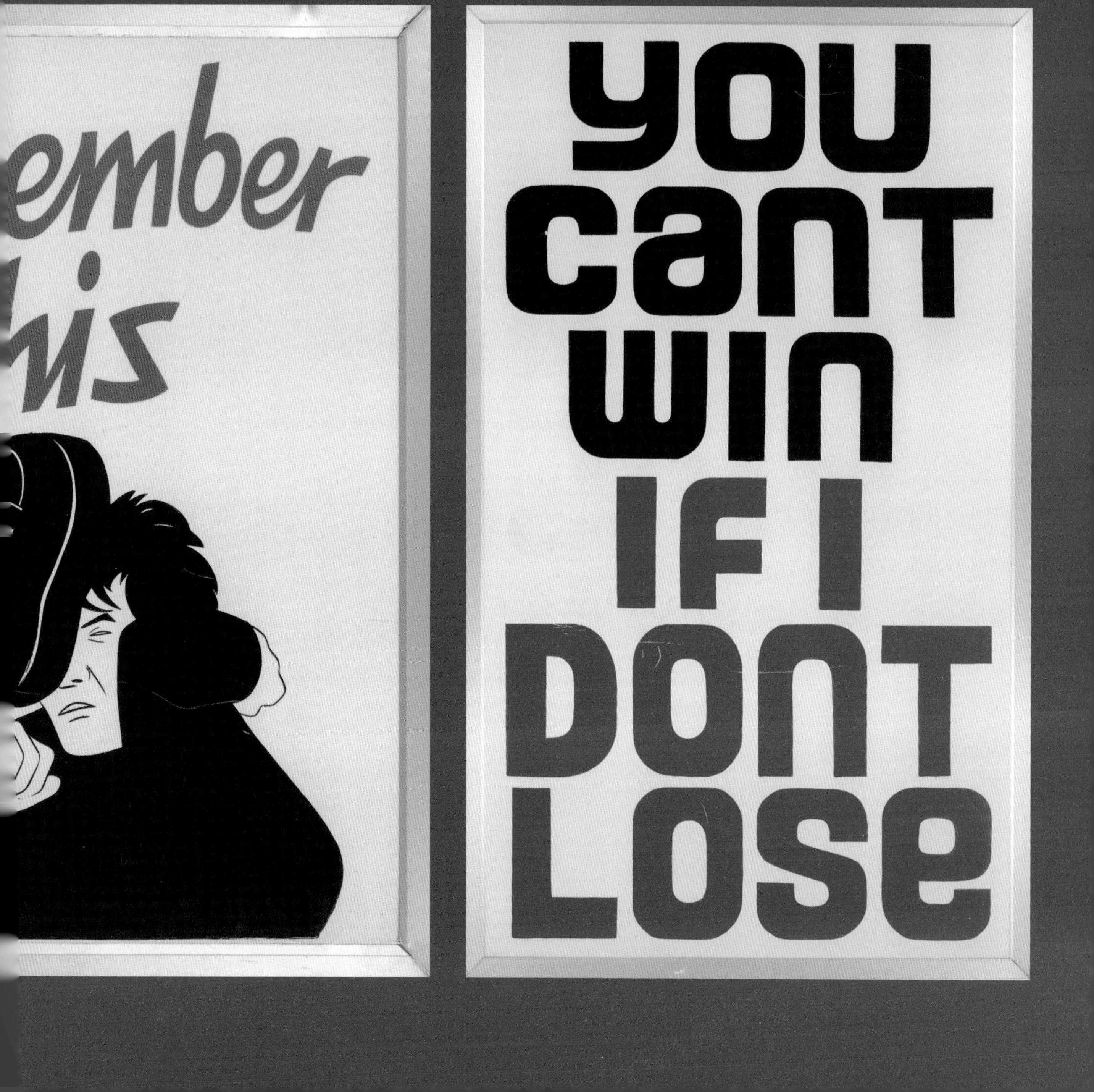
YOU
CANT
WIN
IF I
DONT
LOSE

LOOK!

5

MUTUAL FUNDS

O THE FULLEST EXTENT
OF THE LAW!
– MGR

PIGEON

FOUND!

BLUE VELCRO NO I.D. NO
MONEY, NO CREDIT CARD

F
21
HA
MO
CA

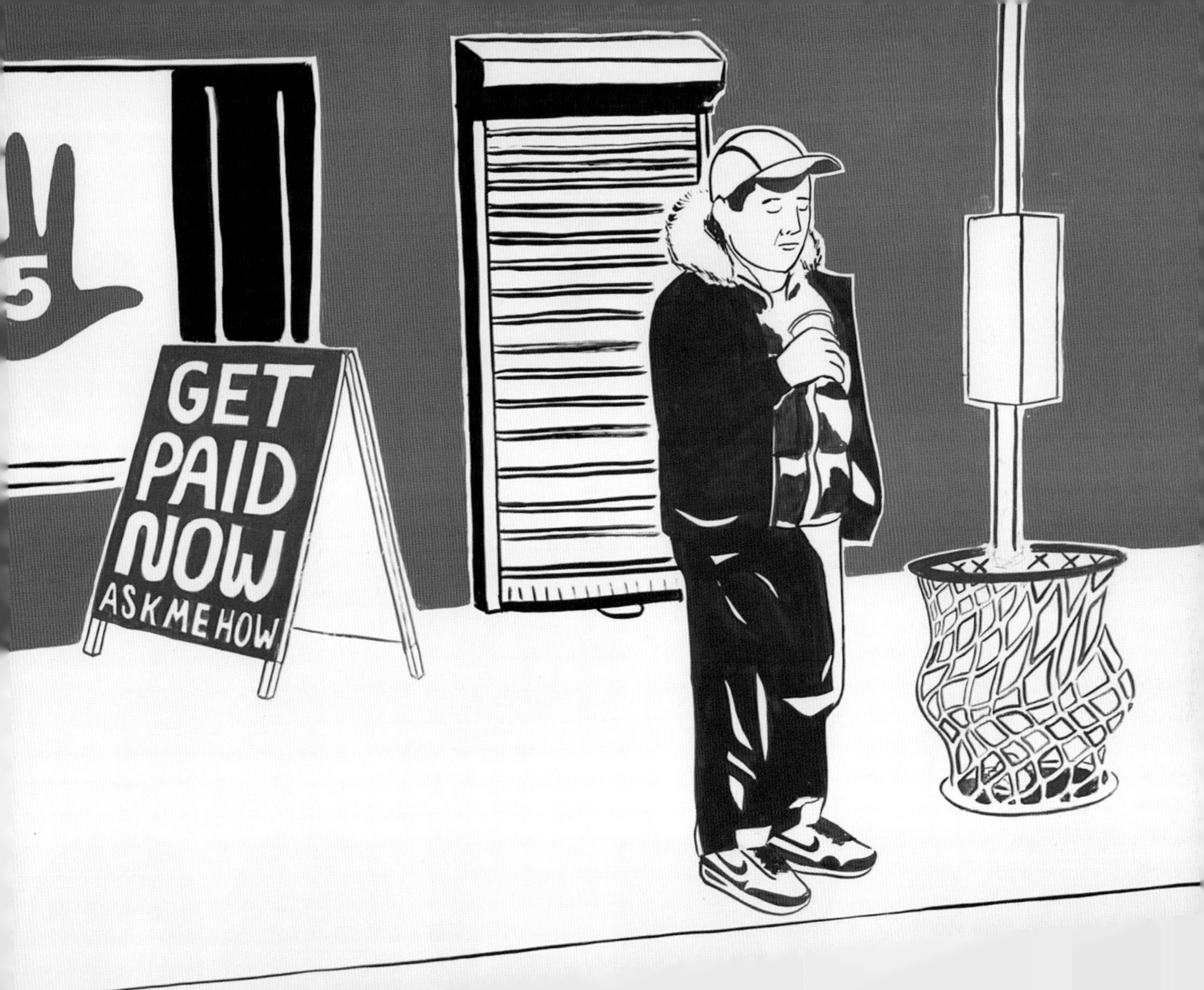
5
GET
PAID
NOW
ASK ME HOW

I BEG
your
pardon

LET ME TALK AT YOU

HE HAD
A KNOT

MY FAMILY IS WAITING FOR ME

AT JABLUKEY
STREET
CHURCH

Take Me
There

FINE

I'LL PUT YOURS WITH MINE

I GOTTA TAKE A LEAK OKAY

SPECIAL !

6

SUPERFEEN WASTES THE DAY
AND SAVES THE NIGHT

O THE FULLEST EXTENT
OF THE LAW!
–MGR

PIGEON

LOST

NEW YORK

REWARD

F

2

HA

MO

CA

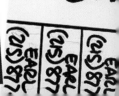

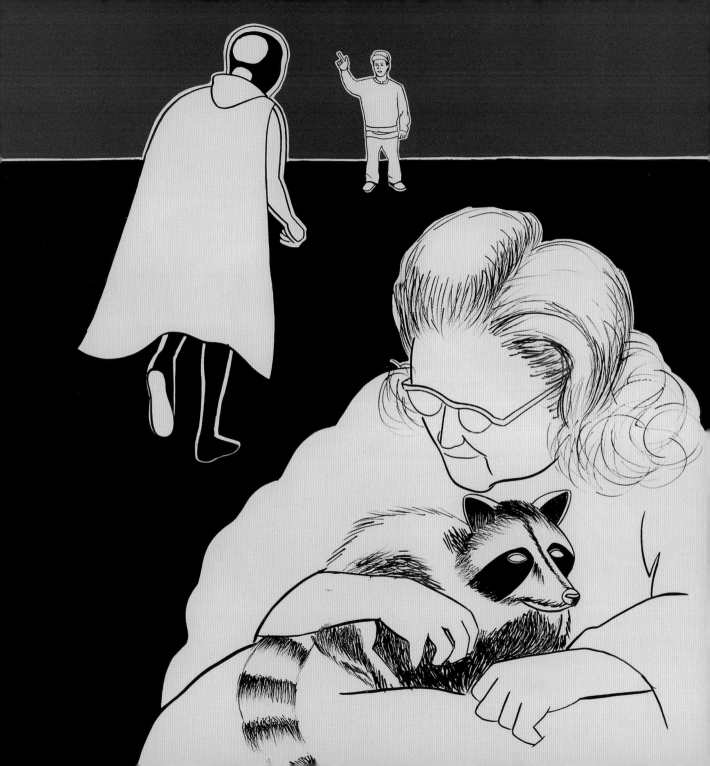

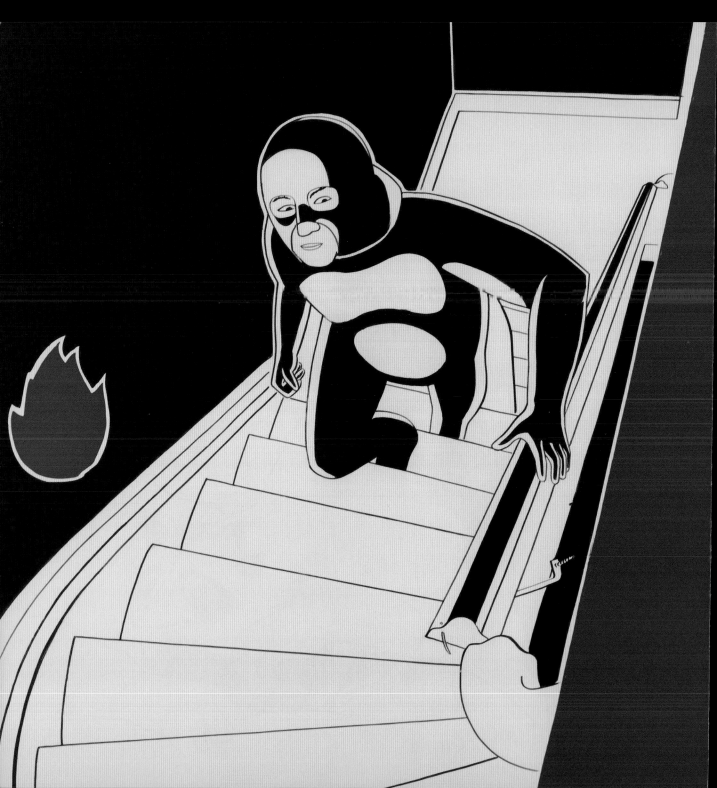

LOOK!

7
FORTRESS

O THE FULLEST EXTENT
OF THE LAW!
— MGR

PIGEON

MISSING

5'11 RED CAPE, BOOTS
ANSWERS TO "HEY YOU"

F
2 L
HAN
MO
CA

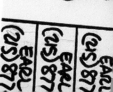

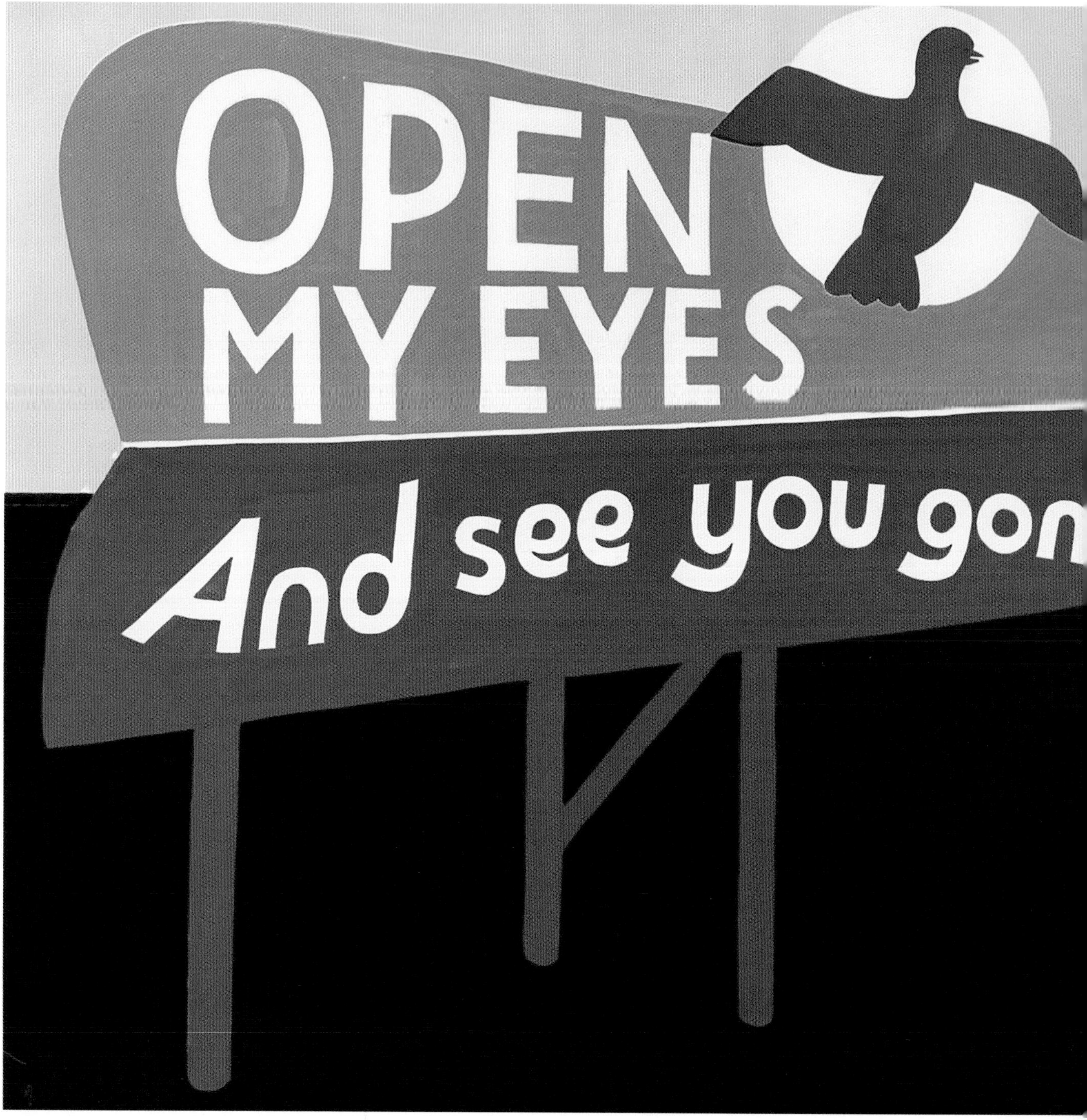
OPEN
MY EYES
And see you gon

SPECIAL !

8

ENDZONE DANCER

O THE FULLEST EXTENT
OF THE LAW!

−MGR

PIGEON

DON'T FEED THE

PIGEONS

F
2 L
HA
MO

CA

EARL
(215) 877
EARL
(215) 877
EARL
(215) 87

QUITTING TIME

THE SIGNS WERE EVERYWHERE

HELP WANTED

ON THE PLUS SIDE

IT'S → HAPPY HOUR

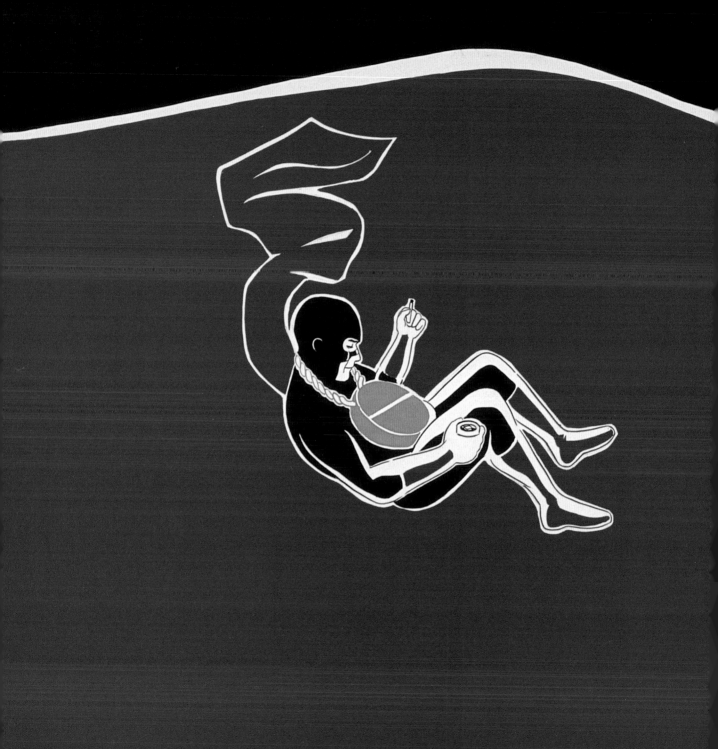

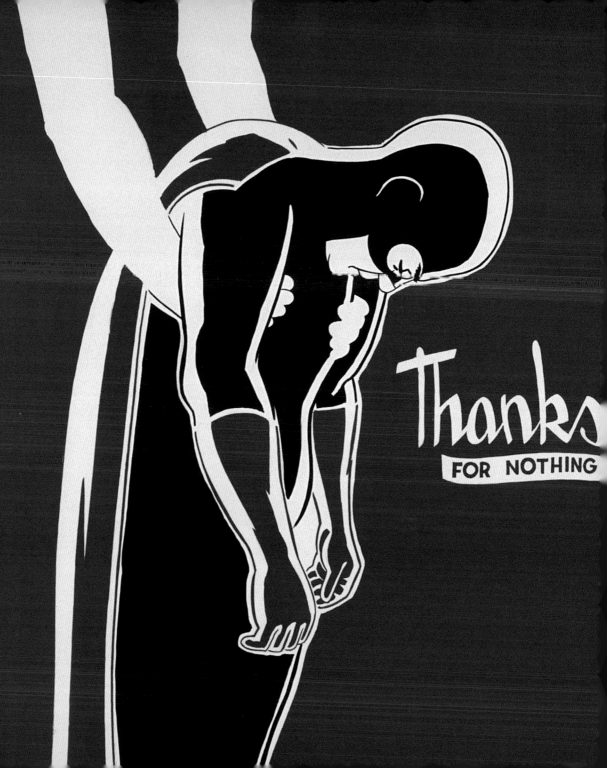

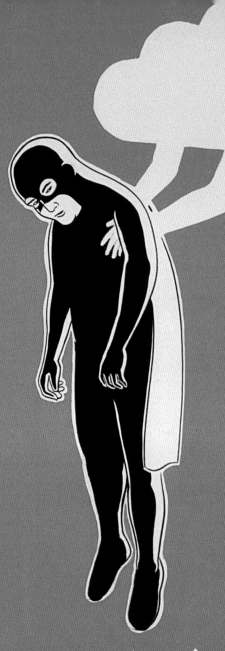

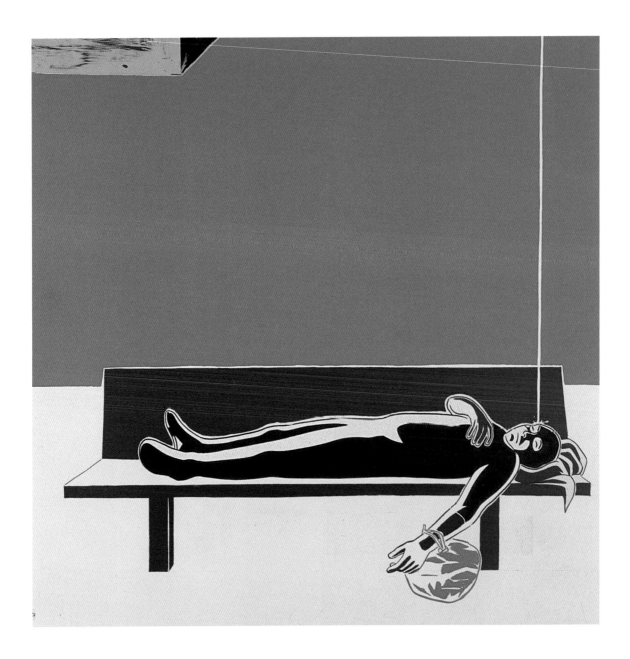

STEVE POWERS was born and raised in Philadelphia. In 1994 he moved to New York City, where he published *On the Go* magazine, authored the book *The Art of Getting Over,* and wrote enough graffiti to get a six-count felony indictment, courtesy of the People of New York. After copping a plea and serving five days of community service, Powers started his studio practice in 1998. Since then he has shown at Deitch Projects, the 49th Venice Biennale, the Luggage Store, and the 2002 Liverpool Biennial. Powers was commissioned to create artwork for the Teen Health Center of the Cincinnati Children's Hospital Medical Center, which was dedicated in October 2002. In 2004 he worked with Creative Time on the Dreamland Artist Club, a project that featured twenty artists painting signs and rides at New York's fabled Coney Island. He lives and works in Manhattan.